Things I Like

I Like Soccer

By Meg Gaertner

level 1
little blue readers

www.littlebluehousebooks.com

Copyright © 2020 by Little Blue House, Mendota Heights, MN 55120. All rights reserved. No part of this book may be reproduced or utilized in any form or by any means without written permission from the publisher.

Little Blue House is distributed by North Star Editions:
sales@northstareditions.com | 888-417-0195

Produced for Little Blue House by Red Line Editorial.

Photographs ©: FatCamera/iStockphoto, cover, 8–9, 15; SeventyFour/iStockphoto, 4; Lorado/iStockphoto, 7; fotokostic/iStockphoto, 10–11; Steve Debenport/iStockphoto, 12–13, 16 (bottom right); solidcolours/iStockphoto, 16 (top left); Jeffoto/iStockphoto, 16 (top right); sharpshutter/iStockphoto, 16 (bottom left)

Library of Congress Control Number: 2019908247

ISBN
978-1-64619-014-0 (hardcover)
978-1-64619-053-9 (paperback)
978-1-64619-092-8 (ebook pdf)
978-1-64619-131-4 (hosted ebook)

Printed in the United States of America
Mankato, MN
012020

About the Author

Meg Gaertner enjoys reading, writing, dancing, and being outside. She lives in Minnesota.

Table of Contents

I Like Soccer 5

Glossary 16

Index 16

ball

I Like Soccer

Soccer is fun.

I play with a ball.

Soccer is fun.

I play in a game.

7

Soccer is fun.

I play on a team.

9

Soccer is fun.

I play on a field.

field

Soccer is fun.

I play by a net.

net

Soccer is fun.

I play with my friends.

15

Glossary

ball

net

field

team

Index

B
ball, 5

G
game, 6

N
net, 12

T
team, 14